THE WOLFSONG SERIES

The
Mysterious
Island

For Jane Marshall and Albert Marshall, whose kind words about my work in the late 1970s helped me become a more ambitious writer.

And to the children and staff at San Tumas More Middle School, Tarxien, in Malta who work and live only a stone's throw away from the mysterious temples in this story. – S.P.

To my little Alice. – D.O.

Wolfsong: The Mysterious Island
An original concept by author Saviour Pirotta
© Saviour Pirotta

Illustrations by Davide Ortu
Represented by Beehive Illustration
www.beehiveillustration.com

Published by MAVERICK ARTS PUBLISHING LTD
Studio 11, City Business Centre, 6 Brighton Road,
Horsham, West Sussex, RH13 5BB
+44 (0) 1403 256941
© Maverick Arts Publishing Limited January 2021

A CIP catalogue record for this book is available
at the British Library.

ISBN: 978-1-84886-700-0

THE WOLFSONG SERIES

The MYSTERIOUS ISLAND

SAVIOUR PIROTTA

ILLUSTRATED BY
DAVIDE ORTU

CONtents

CHAPTER 1   The Cave of Bones

CHAPTER 2   The Prophecy

CHAPTER 3   The Amulet

CHAPTER 4   The Sea Spirit

CHAPTER 5   Carver

CHAPTER 6   To Another Land

CHAPTER 7   A New Kind of Knife

CHAPTER 8   Fire-Mountain

CHAPTER 9   Hard Work

CHAPTER 10   Buried Alive!

CHAPTER 11   Across the Sea

CHAPTER 12   The Mysterious Island

CHAPTER 13   Abandoned Temples

CHAPTER 14   The Bee Children

CHAPTER 15   Rain

CHAPTER 16   Wolfsong

The Whispering
Stones
(Stone Henge)

The Cave of
Dancing Animals
(Lascaux, France)

THE JOURNEY

The Growling
Island (Sicily, Italy)

Fire-Mountain
(Mount Etna)

The Island at the Centre
of the World (Malta)

Chapter 1
The Cave of Bones

'Wolf, did you hear what I said?'

I opened my eyes to see my friend, Crow, glaring down at me. Her long black hair dangled around my face like a curtain.

I was snug under my fur blanket. Shadow, my dog, was tucked in beside me. It was so warm, I was reluctant to stretch out my arms. The hut I was sleeping in looked cosy, with the coals from the fire still glowing in the middle of the room, but I knew they wouldn't be giving out much heat at this time of night.

'I said I spotted Rain,' hissed Crow, shaking me by the shoulder.

That piece of news made me sit up. Shadow growled softly. 'You saw Rain? Where?'

'In the forest,' replied Crow. 'I was chasing a hare and I saw him walking along the forest path with an older woman. That Primrose was with them. They seemed to be in a hurry and determined not to be seen, if you ask me. The woman kept glancing backwards but she seemed to know where she was heading. I nearly hurled my spear at Rain but I stopped myself in time.'

I wouldn't have blamed Crow if she had thrown a spear at Rain. He had caused us a lot of trouble. He'd even tried to kill me. More than once!

Crow, Rain and I all came from the same part of the world, a group of rocky islands where it seems to rain every day and the cold winters last for most of the year. Rain and I have never got on. Once, he accused me of helping Crow steal a sacred spear from our burial mound. It was a false accusation. The spear had actually been stolen by another shaman. But even when I set off on a perilous journey and brought the spear back, he refused to apologise. He continued to stir up vicious rumours, and make fun of me in public.

But it got dramatically worse when I told his father, Moon, that I wanted to be a shaman. Rain had hoped to follow in his father's footsteps, but the village shaman had revealed that the spirits favoured me instead. That made Rain insanely jealous.

Things came to a head when Moon invited me to assist him in a secret ceremony. Rain tried to poison me but, in a bizarre twist of fate, he ended up poisoning his own father. Luckily the old shaman had not died, but the poison had left him ill and weak beyond his years. He had to embark on a long journey to a place of healing, the sanctuary of the Whispering Stones, to ask the spirits for their help. Crow and I went with him and, unbeknown to us, Rain had followed with a group of his equally cruel friends. They'd tried to kill me again and I only survived with the help of the invisible spirits who protect me.

Worst of all, I'd had to sell a valuable amulet whose power sent me dreams that foretold the future. They were dreams whose warnings I was still learning to interpret. Somehow the precious amulet I sold wound up in Rain's hands. I hated to think what he would do with it. Trade it for some dangerous weapon perhaps? Or try to use it himself? Rain liked people to think he was clever and powerful. I was determined to get the amulet back, out of the hands of someone who would abuse it.

'Do you think Rain and his guide saw you?' I asked Crow.

Crow smiled wryly. 'I'm only ever seen when I choose to be. But I did see your amulet hanging on a leather string around his thick neck.'

'Were Rain's other friends with him?' I asked.

'Only Primrose,' said Crow. 'The others seem to have disappeared. I followed Rain to a cave deep in the forest. There was a curtain of dried creeper across the mouth but I could see the glow of a fire through it. I guess the cave is the old woman's home. I hid behind a bush and listened. They had something to eat. Rain's eating habits are so disgusting, you could hear him belching from outside. When he came out for a breath of fresh air, I thought it might be a good idea to jump him but a man turned up. He was so heavily wrapped in fur you could easily have mistaken him for a bear. He turned out to be the woman's son and she came out to greet him. They spent a long time talking, but in the end they put out the fire and went to bed. When I heard them snoring, I decided to come and fetch you.'

'I wonder who the woman is,' I said. 'And why she hides away in the forest. Most people prefer to live in a village, where people can protect each other. Where did Rain meet her, I wonder?'

Crow had no answers. Now that Rain had tried to kill me in front of witnesses, he would not dare return home to Great Island. Of that I was certain.

My people can be hostile to would-be killers, especially ones who attack members of their own tribe. Punishments can be severe.

'But where is he going next?' I wondered out loud.

'The only way to find out is to go after him,' said Crow. 'We don't have a moment to lose.' She started packing her belongings in her fur blanket—arrowheads, spare clothes and flints for making fire.

I started doing the same. 'Should we say goodbye to Moon?' I asked. I threw a glance at the shaman, who was asleep by the fire. His face was lined with the pain and worry of the last few days.

'Let him sleep,' said Crow. 'I'll wake up Sky and tell him.'

Sky was our host. He and his wife, Earth, had let us stay with them while we visited the Whispering Stones. I looked as they slept soundly on the other side of the fire. They seemed completely at peace, and I thought of my own mother and father asleep around their own fire back on Great Island. Did they miss me, I wondered? Did they ask the spirits to watch over me like they had promised?

Crow shook Sky awake. 'Wolf and I are going after Rain,' she whispered.

'So early?' mumbled Sky, wiping the sleep from his eyes.

Crow nodded. 'Tell Moon to wait for us here.'

'And please look after him,' I added, hauling my bundle onto my shoulder. Shadow, realising we were setting off, pattered over to the wooden door.

'The spirits go with you,' said Sky, 'and may they protect you from harm.'

Crow and I slipped out into a cold, misty night, which made me shiver. The mist in the land around the Whispering Stones was very different from the fog on my island. Back home, it was thick. It looked almost like fire smoke, and was so cold it seeped through your furs. Here, the mist was lighter and damper. It clung to your face almost like fine, sticky cobwebs, making you wish you could brush it away.

Crow marched down the narrow path between the houses. There was absolutely no one around. I wasn't surprised. People are scared of mist, no matter how thick or thin it is. They think it harbours night-spirits, the kind that could lead you astray into the dangers of the dark. If I'm honest, it gives me the creeps too, but I had no choice but to venture out.

'Follow me,' said Crow, adjusting the wooden bow on her shoulder.

We left the village and followed a narrow path into the forest. Shadow kept stopping to sniff at the ground or to growl at the darkness in the trees. In the village, it had been quiet but here in the forest, the night was full of sounds. Owls hooted, animal paws scratched at the trees and dried leaves crunched underfoot. Along the path, we spotted ancient trees with bone offerings dangling from their branches. We passed a small circle of standing stones draped with flowery garlands.

'Are you sure we're going the right way?' I asked Crow.

'I left marks on the tree trunks,' she said. 'Just to make sure.'

The trees seemed to grow closer together as we moved deeper into the forest. Before long, we were picking our way between enormous boulders covered in springy moss. Prickly bushes jabbed at my arms and I was glad of my thick, furry boots that stopped the thorns from getting to my legs.

The bushes around us glowed with a strange yellow light.

'Are they night-spirits?' I gasped. 'Careful, they might be dangerous.'

'Don't be silly,' replied Crow. 'You see danger in the

most harmless things.'

She scooped up something from the bush and held it gently towards me. Tiny creatures with fire in their tails were crawling around in her cupped hands.

'See?' she laughed, gently tipping the creatures back into the bush. 'They're beautiful. Nothing to be scared of. Come on, hurry up.'

We came to a shallow stream where Shadow lapped up some water, and picked our way across a long line of stepping stones.

On the opposite bank, Crow put a finger to her lips. 'We need to be quiet here. The cave's just over there.'

She pointed to what looked like a giant crack in a cliff-face. A thick curtain of leaves grew across it. Behind the leaves was complete darkness. I could hear loud snoring.

'That must be Rain,' I said unkindly. 'Only he can snore loud enough to wake the day-spirits.'

'This might be the perfect time to get your

amulet back,' said Crow. 'I could sneak in and lift it off Rain's neck while he snores.'

'If you're going in the cave, I'm coming with you,' I insisted.

She smiled kindly. 'It'll be easier on my own. You stay out here and make sure Shadow doesn't bark. I'll be back before you know it.'

'No,' I argued, following her to the cave. 'I am done with being a coward. I want to get my amulet back myself.'

'Very well,' said Crow. 'Perhaps it is important for a man to prove how brave he is. But I'm coming with you in case you need help.'

I knelt and rubbed my thumbs between Shadow's ears. 'You wait for us here, boy. No noise now, do you hear?'

Shadow wagged his tail to show he understood. Crow parted the curtain of leaves and we slipped into the cave. There was a terrible stench of rotting meat and smoking peat. A clammy heat stuck to my skin. As the curtain closed behind me, I stood as still as a standing stone and tried to make out my surroundings.

The cave was full of animal skeletons, piled high against the walls. The bones glowed a soft white in the dark, as if they had been licked clean. Had their spirits been thanked properly for giving up their life, I wondered? The skulls glared at me with hollow eyes. They made my skin crawl and I wished I had my precious amulet to protect me.

Crow nudged me gently and I dragged my eyes away from the bones to the back of the cave. There were four sleeping figures huddled under fur blankets, two close to the smoking peat and two further back in the cave.

I recognised Rain right away because his enormous boots were sticking out from under his blanket. He grunted in his sleep as I edged closer, holding my breath. I could see my amulet hanging around his neck. It was so near—all I had to do was reach over and cut it free.

I was feeling under my belt for my flint knife

when one of the other blankets twitched.

Someone raised their head. I froze.

'Son, is that you? Is it time to get up already?'

It was the woman. I ducked, hoping that she wouldn't see me.

'Son?' She waited for an answer but when none came she lowered her head on the floor again. Only for a moment though. Before I even had time to move, she threw back her fur blanket and got to her feet. I lay very still, my heart thumping wildly in my chest as the woman

shuffled right past me to the entrance of the cave. She disappeared outside.

'Wolf!' Crow hissed at me from behind a pile of bones. 'Forget about getting the amulet. Get over here, quick.'

I barely had time to scurry across the floor towards her before the woman returned. She threw fresh peat on the fire, poked it with a stick, then went over to her son and shook him gently.

'Get up, Oak. We need to get going.'

Her son grunted and turned over. 'Do we need

to go so early?'

'We can't risk anyone seeing us.'

'We're in the middle of a forest. No one ever comes here.'

'It's best to be sure. Wake the boy and the girl up.'

Oak stumbled to his feet, lumbered over to Rain and patted him on the shoulder. 'Get up,' he hissed. 'Mother says we need to get going right away.'

'But I'm still tired,' whined Rain.

'You want to become a shaman, don't you?' said Oak impatiently. 'Isn't that what you said last night? Well, get up. We are going to see someone who can make you the most important shaman in the world.'

ChapteR 2
The Prophecy

I watched from my hiding place as Rain got up and started bundling up his belongings. He tucked my amulet under his tunic. Again, I felt a wave of hot anger sweep across my face, but I knew there was nothing I could do.

The woman shook Primrose awake.

'Come on, little one. We have a long journey ahead of us.'

Primrose sat up reluctantly. 'Are we going then?'

The woman nodded. 'Yes. I'm bringing food with us so hurry up and I'll give you something to eat on the road.' They trooped out of the cave while I prayed Rain wouldn't spot Shadow outside.

As the curtain of leaves fell back in place, Crow turned to me. 'Look at these,' she said. 'I found them among these piles of bones. They're deer skulls with large antlers. You can wear them on your head.'

'What for?' I asked.

'If you were following deer on a hunt, they'd make a good disguise,' she said. 'If your prey got wind of you, you could crouch in the grass and pretend you're a deer. I think it's very clever. Put one on. I'm going to. They'll help us follow Rain undetected.'

We slipped through the curtain and quickly caught sight of Rain and his companions.

They led us deeper into the forest until we came to a part of it where the thick branches of the trees met overhead. It was so dark, you could easily imagine that it was always night-time here. I saw a light burning in the distance. Getting closer, I realised it was coming from a strange building made of standing stones. They formed a tight circle. The doorposts sloped, so that the entrance was wider at the bottom than at the top. The light was shining from inside it.

All the buildings I'd ever seen in my life had roofs made of straw or wood but this one was topped with enormous stones whose ends jutted out over the walls. But that wasn't the most striking thing about the place. Suspended on long strings from the branches of the trees above, were clusters of lamps. Their light flickered in the breeze so that the building looked as if it were permanently standing under a cloudless, starlit sky.

There was movement in the doorway and a tall man came out. He opened his arms to welcome Rain, Primrose and their adult companions. 'Greetings. This is Her temple,' he said. 'I am Starlight, the shaman.'

So this building was called a temple. I wondered what its function was. Did anyone live in it? It was certainly big enough to house an entire village. Perhaps people came here to pay their respect to the spirits, or to honour their dead ancestors. But why was it hidden so deep in the forest? Who would build a place so difficult to get to?

A girl about my age appeared in the doorway, holding a small bowl in her outstretched hands. Starlight dipped his fingers in it and touched the visitors' foreheads. I was too far away to see properly but I guessed he was painting some kind of mark or symbol.

'She Who Sleeps welcomes you,' he said, then turned to Rain. 'Is this the young man you mentioned?'

The woman nodded. 'It is. Eh!'

'She Who Sleeps awaits,' said Starlight. 'Come.'

Rain and the others followed, the light inside the temple throwing long shadows on the grass as they entered. When their voices had faded, I turned to Crow. 'This is all very mysterious,' I said. 'Who is She Who Sleeps?'

'I have no idea,' replied Crow. 'But we're certainly going to find out. Follow me.'

We hid the antlers behind a bush and hurried across the grass towards the temple, Shadow panting at my feet. The doorway led into a narrow corridor lined with burning torches. On either side, the stone walls were decorated with beautifully drawn animals. There were bulls, fattened pigs and even geese with enormous, sharp beaks. They were all painted in a deep red that looked like blood in the flickering light. Every animal was walking in the same direction, deeper into the strange temple.

We turned a corner and the corridor sloped downward, round and round in an ever-tightening circle. It was taking us deep into the ground. Now the animals on the walls were replaced by a flowing pattern of circles, like enormous waves on a stormy sea.

Crow signalled at me to hurry up and we soon heard a familiar voice. Ahead of us, the light got brighter. The corridor gave out into a wide, round room but we hung back in the shadows. Rain and

Starlight were sitting on stone seats in the middle of the room. All around, the walls were covered in the same red circles as the corridor.

Now that I could see Starlight properly, I noticed that his hair was longer than Crow's. His head was shaved at the front so that he looked like an old man who was going bald.

'I was lucky to meet your friends, sir,' said Rain, gesturing to Oak and his mother who were standing nearby. 'They told me all about you.'

'We only spoke because we saw the amulet hanging round his neck, master,' said the woman nervously. 'We are not in the habit of revealing our sacred secrets.' She nudged Rain. 'Boy, tell him what you told us.'

'They speak the truth,' said Rain. He was using a false tone of voice I'd never heard him use before—sort of meek and polite. It set my teeth on edge.

'I was on the road, thanking the spirits, when this woman walked by and noticed the amulet I was holding up to the skies.'

'Eh,' confirmed the woman. 'I couldn't help noticing it was shaped like a bird's head, just like in the prophecy. Boy, show him.'

Rain reached inside his furs and pulled out my bird-skull amulet.

Starlight looked at it for a long while but made no attempt to touch it. 'Who gave it to you?'

'My beloved father,' said Rain.

'And who is your father?'

'A well-respected shaman,' answered Rain. 'I live on an island in the distant north. It was clear to my father, even when I was still a small child, that I was destined to become a shaman like him.'

I nearly gasped out loud when I heard these terrible lies but Crow put a hand firmly on my shoulder.

'And why have you travelled so far from your land?' asked Starlight.

'Last winter, my father was poisoned by a jealous boy in our village,' said Rain, pretending to sob with grief. 'He is my rival and will do just about anything to become the village shaman instead of me.'

Had Crow not been holding me back, I would have leapt out to confront Rain. How dare he accuse someone else of a crime he himself had committed?

'We travelled to the famous Whispering Stones, hoping the spirits would make my father better,' he went on. 'Sadly, it was not to be. We buried Father only a few days ago.'

'Aye,' said Primrose, joining in with the sheer lies. 'I saw the old shaman die with my own eyes. Racked with pain he was, towards the end.'

'Poor, poor child,' sobbed the woman. 'To lose your father at your age.' Oak glared at her to make her be quiet.

'But the Whispering Stones revealed something to me about my future,' continued Rain.

'And what did the stones tell you?' asked Starlight.

'That I would soon meet a man from the stars,' answered Rain without hesitation. 'He would help me become the shaman my father wanted me to be. I guess, sir, if your name is Starlight, you must be the one. Will you help me fulfil my father's wish?'

'My ancestors too come from a place a long way away from here,' said Starlight. 'But it is far to the south, where the sun shines warm most of the year and the land is green in the winter rather than the summer. People call it the Island at the Centre of the World. If you agree to return there with me, I could help you fulfil your father's wish.'

'I will,' said Rain, trying his best to sound humble. 'Perhaps my actions will please my late father's spirit. But there is one thing that scares me. I was followed here by the jealous boy who murdered my father. I am afraid he intends to kill me too. Perhaps, if I gave you his description, you might be able to stop him. He travels with a fierce-looking girl.'

'Fear not, my men will protect you from him,' growled Starlight.

'They must be careful,' warned Rain. 'The boy looks meek but he is ruthless. He has even dared to steal my name.'

'And what is your name?' asked Starlight.

Rain answered without batting an eyelid. 'My name is Wolf.'

Chapter 3
The Amulet

I was speechless with anger. Rain had stolen my name. He'd turned me into the criminal and himself into the victim.

Crow's grip tightened on my shoulder. I saw her eyes flashing in the dark. *Don't do anything foolish*, they seemed to warn me.

Starlight stood up. 'You shall be watched over by my men every step of the journey. Your enemy will not be able to get near you, let alone harm you.'

Rain beckoned Primrose forward. 'My friend has travelled with me from the far north and has protected me from the boy who wants to kill me.

We must take her with us.'

'If that is what you desire,' said Starlight. 'But come, we must offer sacrifice to She Who Sleeps. We have kept her waiting long enough.'

Several men appeared in the room from other doorways and opened a trapdoor in the floor. Starlight took a torch and led the way down deeper into the ground. After a while, I heard the sound of drums and people chanting.

'Come on,' whispered Crow. 'We've seen enough. Let's get out of here before we're discovered.'

We hurried back along the narrow corridor, Shadow trotting ahead of us.

'How dare he?' I hissed once we were out in the open. 'It's like he is stealing my very spirit.'

'He's playing a very dangerous game,' Crow said to calm me down. 'But don't worry, we'll soon sort him out.'

'But how?' I asked.

'We shall capture Rain and bring him back

home to face justice.'

'I have no idea how we're going to manage that,' I said. 'Starlight has promised him that he'll be guarded day and night. I will have to ask the spirits for guidance. Perhaps they will show us the way.'

Crow retrieved the antlers from their hiding place in the bush. 'Starlight's men don't scare me,' she said confidently. 'Let them try and lay a finger on either of us. Come on, if we're crafty enough, we'll nab Rain before he gets to the sea.'

We'd barely finished talking when voices echoed at the temple doorway. Crow quickly pulled me behind a tree. Starlight emerged with Rain and the others in tow. He was swaddled in thick furs for the journey, as were Rain, Primrose and the men we'd seen in the temple. I held Shadow's mouth closed as they passed by. He still managed to growl but, thankfully, no one heard him.

Crow and I followed at a distance, wearing our

antlers. We came to the woman's cave where they all disappeared inside. Squeezing inside a hollow tree, we kept watch. Soon the smell of roasting meat wafted out and my stomach growled with hunger.

Crow pulled some dried meat from her bundle. It was tough as old fur but I was grateful for it and gave some to Shadow. I had no idea how long we spent inside that tree, shivering with cold, but at last Rain and Starlight came out of the cave again, followed by their men. Oak and his mother waved from the entrance.

'May you have a safe journey.'

'She Who Sleeps will protect us,' replied Starlight. 'We are grateful for the delicious meal, and the food for our journey. May the spirits repay your kindness many times over.'

'Hurry up, Wolf,' whispered Crow and we took off after them. They were using the forest path so we kept to the undergrowth, which was thick and provided good cover. Still, I had to admit, it felt good having the antlers on my head, even if they did make me feel ridiculous.

The path led to rolling hills where land had been cleared for farming. It seemed to stretch on forever and I lost track of time as we followed Rain. One day followed another. We passed a few small villages, some of them ringed with stone walls for safety, others protected only with wooden fences. Rain, Primrose and Starlight always stopped and begged a bed for the night but Crow and I remained concealed in the fields with Shadow always on the lookout for strangers.

Most nights, Crow went hunting while I made a fire and sharpened my flint knife. We were always careful to have our fire well hidden in case someone saw the smoke and came to investigate.

Tucked up in my furs at night, I often wished I still had my amulet. Perhaps it would give me another seeing-dream and show me how to capture Rain.

As we progressed further south, the landscape

changed yet again. The ground turned into soft, white rock. It had tiny shells embedded in it. You could carve them out with a sharp flint knife.

Not that I inspected the ground much. I always kept an eye on Rain and I soon discovered a pattern in his behaviour. Every evening, he would sit near the fire and make a great show of holding my amulet to his forehead, as if it was passing secret messages to him. But the moment the grown ups' backs were turned, he and Primrose would start playing a childish game with pebbles.

'If only we could find him alone for one moment,' sighed Crow impatiently one night as Rain sat with the others under a tree. 'We could whisk him away before Starlight and his men even realised something was going on.'

'He might not be favoured by the spirits, but he's no fool,' I answered. 'He'll always stick close to Starlight's men.'

A few days later, we came to a forest on a cliff. Beyond it, I could make out a rolling sea, dark as flint. My heart sank when I saw it. Once Rain got on a boat, we stood no chance of capturing him. We didn't even have a skiff.

'We have to get him today,' I said to Crow, as we found a hiding place between two large rocks in a meadow.

'Don't worry,' said Crow. 'There are no farms around here. They'll have to spend the night out in the open. We'll wait until everyone's asleep and then we'll creep up on them.'

'But how can we grab Rain without waking the others up?' I asked.

'Look at these pink flowers,' said Crow, indicating to the meadow around us. 'They grow on my island too.'

'And mine,' I said.

'We dig up the roots to make sleeping potions,' said Crow. 'I could make one and slip it in their food. They won't even stir as we drag Rain away.'

I peeped round the boulder to see Rain and his friends had set up camp under a tree. They had a fire going and one of the men was pouring oats into a large cooking pot.

'They're making porridge,' I said.

Crow grinned as she dug up roots with her fingers. 'Perfect. I'll create a diversion so you can sneak up through the grass and pour the sleeping potion into the pot.'

'What kind of diversion?' I asked.

Crow giggled. 'You'll see.'

She ground the scraggly roots with a flat stone and mixed it with water from her flask to make a potion. As the sun set, flooding the world with orange light, she crept through the grass until she was on the other side of the tree. I watched with bated breath as a pair of antlers reared up above the ferns.

'Look, a deer,' I heard Primrose shout right away.

Rain was the first to reach for his spear. 'Come on, let's get it. I could do with some nice juicy meat.'

The others followed, leaving the cooking pot unattended. Seeing my chance, I crept through the grass. Reaching the pot, I poured in the sleeping potion. The men had left the stirring stick nearby and I wondered if I should give it a good stir, to make sure the potion reached every bit of the porridge. But I didn't dare risk it. One of the men might come back anytime.

'Let's get away,' I whispered to Shadow, who had followed me. We crept through the grass again

and waited
for Crow in our
hiding place. When she returned
some time later, a big smile was on her face.

'These antlers are coming in handy in all sorts
of ways,' she said. 'Well done for putting the
sleeping potion in the food.'

'It must have been quite strong,' I said. 'Listen,
they're snoring already.'

Crow grinned wider. 'Come on. Get your
things. We need to be as far away as possible
when it wears off.'

We ran towards the tree where the men were
all lying on the ground, their mouths wide open.

Crow and I rolled Rain onto a fur blanket and dragged him away.

The moment we were clear of the others, we stopped and tied Rain's hands and feet together. While Crow gagged him with a strip of fur, I felt inside his tunic. My fingers closed around the amulet and, I was so eager to get it back, I pulled it off so hard the thong broke. My blood thumped in my head with triumph. I tied a new knot on the leather thong and slipped the amulet over my head.

'I thank the spirits for letting me get it back,' I said.

'Good,' replied Crow. 'But look, the blanket is leaving a trail in the grass. When Starlight and his men wake up, it will lead them straight to us.'

She looked around. 'Let's find a branch. One thick and strong enough to take Rain's weight.'

With Rain lashed to the branch by the wrists and ankles, we set off like hunters bringing home prey. Crow suggested we walk along the edge of the cliff where the bare rocks would show no footprints. The wind was quite strong, threatening to blow us off the cliff, but we made good progress. By the time the sun came up, I reckoned we'd left Starlight and his men far behind. Rain was starting to come round. He looked around him, confused at first, then with anger brimming in his eyes. He squirmed against the ties.

'It's no use,' I said. 'You're tied up like a pig. And I have my amulet back to protect me from you. We're taking you straight back to your father.'

Rain's eyes bulged with fury and he tried to speak through the gag.

'We know what you're trying to say,' said Crow. '"Starlight and his men will catch up with us long before we get back to the Whispering Stones." But you underestimated us. There's nothing that will stop us bringing you to justice. Now stop kicking and growling or I'll have to truss you even tighter.'

The threat made Rain shut up and we struggled on in silence. He seemed to be getting heavier by the moment. The branch dug painfully into my shoulder.

'I can't carry him anymore,' I said to Crow. 'Why don't we cut him loose from the branch? He can't run away if we keep his feet tied together.'

'I don't know,' replied Crow. 'We could perhaps have a rest till you can carry him again.'

'We'll just loosen the ropes round his hands and feet so he can walk but not run. Look, the blood is trapped in his hands. We want to get him back to Moon alive.'

'Very well,' said Crow, although I could sense reluctance in her voice. We stopped and I released Rain from the branch.

'Don't do anything foolish now,' said Crow, as she loosened the rope around Rain's hands and feet. 'One false move, and I'll run you through with my spear.'

Rain said nothing but his eyes narrowed. I knew that look very well. He was thinking hard, weighing up his chances of escape. I wondered if we'd made a mistake cutting him loose from the branch after all. But it was done now and I really could not have carried him another step. My shoulder was in agony.

I prayed to the spirits for their protection. It was only fair they helped me, after all. Wasn't I helping out a broken-hearted father, and righting a terrible wrong that had been done to me?

But sadly the spirits were not on my side that day. As we hurried along the cliff, Shadow stopped dead in his tracks. He whined and pawed at the ground.

'Shadow,' I said. 'Is something the matter?'

A moment later, I could feel the ground give slightly under my feet. Shadow growled.

'I think the rock under our feet is loose,' I said to Crow, looking around me in alarm. 'Let's go back.'

What happened next will live in my memory until the end of my days. I grabbed Crow's hand and tried taking another step, only to feel the ground give way some more. I saw a grin flash across Rain's face. He leapt forward and snatched the amulet right from round my neck. Shadow flew at him but he managed to jump away. Then there was a sound like a crack of lighting and the rock beneath me fell away from the cliff.

I plunged, kicking and screaming, towards the sea below.

CHAPTER 4
The Sea Spirit

I hit the water like a stone. The sea closed over my head and, within moments, I felt my body start to go numb. Darkness swamped my mind and I knew I was going to drown. I can swim but my thick furs were weighing me down. With water filling my mouth, I fancied I saw the spirits reaching out to me from the great beyond.

Then a hand grabbed me by the shoulder and I was pulled upwards, to safety. I spat out the water, gasping like a fish. Shadow barked in my ear and I felt his rough tongue against my cheek.

'Float still for a few moments,' ordered Crow. 'Try and breathe normally. It will calm you down.'

'Did you pull me up to the surface?' I spluttered. 'Or was that the work of the spirits?'

'I'm afraid it was only me,' said Crow. 'Now rest like I said.'

'Where's Rain?' I asked.

'He's still on top of the cliff.'

'Ha,' I sighed, 'the bad spirits truly favour him.'

'He's a quick thinker,' said Crow. 'He saw his chance and grabbed it.'

'What do we do now?' I asked.

'The first thing to do is get out of this water,' answered Crow.

'You mean swim around the cliff till we find a beach?'

Crow shook her head. 'We can't risk that. There might not be anywhere to get out. We'll freeze to death. Look, can you see that rock?

You can wait for me there while I climb up the cliff to try and get help.'

'It's a long climb,' I said.

Crow smiled. 'But I'm very good at climbing cliffs, remember? Come on, let's get to that rock before we go completely numb.'

We reached the rock and I clambered on to it, my teeth chattering with the cold. Crow made me take off my furs. 'Spread them on the ground,' she said. 'They'll dry quicker. See you in a while.'

I watched her clamber up the cliff and disappear over the top. I hoped against hope Rain would not be lying in wait for her. Not that he could do much with both feet tied.

Sitting on that rock with Shadow, I felt anger bubble inside me.

'It's not fair, Shadow,' I said bitterly. 'Rain has my amulet again. Why do the spirits side with him and not me? It should be the other way round. I am the good guy. He is the bad one.'

Shadow licked my hand to cheer me up and I

hugged him close. I was grateful for his company but I was still seething.

All my life I had been afraid of Rain, cowering from his taunts and cruel jokes. Afraid that he would make fun of me in front of the whole village, terrified that he would eventually succeed in hurting me. But now it seemed that I had lost that fear. It was gone, replaced by a deeper, darker feeling.

I hated Rain. I hated him for making my life difficult, for lying about me, for pretending to be me. For trying to kill me.

But the thing that made me the angriest was stealing my precious amulet a second time. The amulet that the dead healer had gifted to *me*.

Deep in my heart, I knew that the amulet was the key to my future. And I wanted it back.

In my village, I was considered the kind, sensitive boy who would not harm a fly. But sitting there in the cold, with the choppy sea lapping at my feet and rain clouds building above me, I did not feel kind anymore. I felt this new dark feeling seeping out of my spirit to fill my entire body.

It was *rage* and it flowed through me like an icy river, filling every part of my being.

I stood up and spat into the water. 'Let that be my offering to the spirit of the sea,' I said out loud. 'Not the generous spirit that gives us fish to eat and carries our skiffs safely home, but the dark spirit that gives life to unseen monsters and drags unlucky people to their death. The dangerous spirit that roars against the cliffs, that smashes boats against the rocks! He will be my companion, and he will help me in my fight against Rain.'

As if in answer, the waves tossed a dead crab at my feet. It had a bright red shell, the colour of blood. Scooping it up, I realised its claws had already gone hard and shrivelled. It stank but I ripped the binding leather from my tunic, poked a hole in the crab with the sharp edge of a stone and hung it round my neck.

Now I had a new amulet. I would carry the

dark spirit of the sea with me wherever I went. It would help me catch up with Rain, no matter how fast he ran, no matter what obstacles he put in my way.

I would bring him back to justice.

I would get my bird-skull amulet back.

'So I have wished,' I roared at the waves. 'So it will happen.'

Chapter 5
Carver

'Greetings!'

The word carried across the water and I looked up to see a skiff approaching. A boy about my age was paddling confidently. I stood up to answer him.

'Am I glad to see you. I'm Wolf and this is my dog, Shadow.'

'Your friend Crow sent me,' said the boy, holding out the paddle to stop his skiff bumping against the rock. 'My name is Shell.'

'Shell?' I asked.

'Yes, my father named me after the shells he picks for necklaces and headdresses. This bit of coast is well known for them.' He held out his hand. 'Now hop on. I can feel the tide starting to rise.'

Even when Shadow was cold and wet, I still had to coax him into Shell's skiff. It seemed his fear of the sea had not quite left him. As I sat down carefully, he licked Shell's hand.

'He's saying thank you,' I said, 'and so do I.'

'Your friend promised me three arrowheads if I came to your rescue,' he said. 'That will be thanks enough. There's another paddle behind you if you want to get to the shore quicker.'

Shell's skiff was tiny but sturdy and we soon skirted round a headland. A sandy beach came into view, with many boats pulled up for safety on the high rocks behind it. Beyond them, I could see a village of stone huts with smoke rising from the roofs. The air was heavy with the smell of fish being smoked.

'If you like fish, our village is the place to be,' joked Shell.

'I'm surprised at how big it is,' I said, 'and how many boats there are. I live close to a fishing village myself, but we have only a few skiffs compared to yours.'

'Ah, but not all the vessels you see are used for fishing,' said Shell. 'Some of them are strong enough to carry people right across the sea to the land down south.'

'What kind of people?' I asked.

'Travellers,' replied Shell. 'People coming or going to the Places of the Living and the Dead, or traders wanting to barter pottery or cloth— although most of those tend to have boats of their own. Many of them speak languages I don't understand. Sometimes they barter goods for my parents' shell necklaces and we are grateful for that.'

Our skiff came to rest in the shallow waters where Crow was waiting.

'It's going to be a cold night,' said Shell. 'Why don't you come to our house for supper? You can barter the meal for anything you have.'

'I have an extra flint knife,' said Crow. 'Will that do?'

'It will indeed,' replied Shell. 'Mother needs a new knife.'

As we ate, Crow told Shell's family about our journey from the Whispering Stones to the coast. She left out the bits about Rain. Instead she told them how the cliff had collapsed under our feet.

'You've had a lucky escape,' said Shell's mother. 'The rocks up there have been crumbling into the sea as long as I can remember. Praise the good spirits.'

'Where are you travelling to?' asked Shell's father.

'I am training to be a shaman,' I said, 'and we are seeking the Island at the Centre of the World.'

Shell's father looked from Crow to me. 'It worries me that you travel alone—two children without an adult to protect you.'

'Don't worry about that,' smiled Crow. 'I can take care of both of us, and we have a fierce dog.'

'You came from the Whispering Stones, the Place of the Dead?' Shell's mother asked.

I nodded. 'Yes.'

'There is another man who came from the same place only this morning. He is staying the night with my sister's family. He is a bit older than you. Perhaps you can share a boat with him tomorrow, since he is headed in the same direction. He could be your guardian.'

'That's a great idea,' I said. 'With a guide, we won't get lost.'

Shell was sent to fetch the young man while his mother brought out hazelnuts for a treat. The man was about my brother Hawk's age, with long black hair tied with a leather thong behind his head. His eyes were very dark and had a kind look to them.

'My name's Carver,' he said, helping himself to some nuts. He spoke my language but with a musical lilt to it.

'What is a carver?' asked Shell.

'I carve stones,' said Carver.

'Do you make amulets for people?' Shell wanted to know.

'No, I help carve enormous rocks. Standing stones.'

'Like the Whispering Stones,' I said.

'Yes, in fact I'm on my way home from there. I helped carve the new stones.' He stopped with a hazelnut halfway to his mouth. 'Wait, I knew I'd seen you somewhere before. You're the boy who was nearly crushed to death when one of the stones toppled over. I was there when it happened.

I say, the spirits must like you, given the way someone pulled you away just in time.'

Shell looked at me with newfound respect in his eyes. 'You were nearly *crushed* by a standing stone? You almost *died?*'

'I just happened to be in the wrong place at the wrong time,' I said hurriedly, not wanting to mention Rain. 'Some children sneaked into the sanctuary and pushed the stone over, just for a dare I should imagine.'

'These two seem to invite danger,' fussed Shell's mother. 'First one of them nearly gets killed by a falling stone, then they fall off a cliff. They're on their way south, to the Island at the Centre of the World. Will you let them travel with you, Carver? At least they will have someone to look after them.'

'I am not travelling as far south as the Island at the Centre of the World,' replied Carver. 'But I am going at least half the way there, to my own village in the Land of Many Colours. They can come with me, if they are willing to share the price of the journey. It will be good to have company.'

'Have you been to the Island at the Centre of the World?' I asked.

'I haven't had the pleasure,' replied Carver. 'But my father says it is a beautiful island. The sun shines all the year round. It is warm even in winter. There are more temples there than in any other place in the world, some of them so ancient, no one knows who built them. But something happened many years ago. The people on the island disappeared. No one knows what became of them or where they went but traders who stop there for fresh water say the place is deserted. The temples stand empty. The houses are falling to ruin. Why do you want to go there, if I may ask?'

'We are looking for someone and we believe he is also on his way to this mysterious island,' I replied. 'When do we set off?'

'I have some preparations to do tomorrow,' he replied. 'We leave at dawn the next morning.'

CHAPTER 6
To Another Land

Shell and his parents stood on the wet sand to wave us goodbye. Our boat was made of tree branches, bent into shape and lashed together with leather rope. It was covered in animal hide rather than fur that, Carver explained, helped it flow better in the water. There were three seats, each one roomy enough to take two people. As there were only five of us—me, Crow, Carver, Shadow and the boatman—there was plenty of room to stretch out.

'It may be roomy, but that also means there are less hands to paddle,' said the boatman, a short man with a balding head and powerful, hairy arms. 'We're all going to have to put our backs to it.'

A stiff breeze helped us along and the shore slowly disappeared behind us. My previous journeys had never taken me out of sight of land. Seeing just open water and sky gave me a strange feeling. Truth be told, I was quite nervous. How did we know in which direction to row? What if we drifted and got lost forever?

'You have nothing to worry about,' laughed Carver, seeing my pale face. 'Journeys across the sea can be quite dangerous but we're in safe hands with Blue, our boatman. He's carried me from one land to another many times.'

I breathed a sigh of relief. I'd known Carver less than two full days but I'd already started to trust him. Perhaps it was because he took so much pride in his work. Most men were only proud of their physical strength and cunning. They liked to boast about the fierce animals they'd killed during a hunt or how cunning they were at bartering.

Carver talked with excitement about turning rocks into things of mystery and beauty, into standing stones. His passion was building temples.

'They are doorways to the invisible world,' he had explained at our evening meal the night before. 'Stand in a temple and you can feel yourself right on the edge, between our world and the other. You can almost reach out and touch the hidden world.'

I had never heard anyone talk so beautifully about the world of the spirits, not even Moon. 'And my work,' Carver went on, 'helps people understand the wonder of the invisible world. Every time I carve a stone, every time someone makes an image on a wall, or a design on a bowl or jug, they are trying to explain the beauty of the world of spirits.'

He pointed to my crab pendant. 'Take this little sea creature. Before you plucked it from the sea, it was only the carcass of a dead animal. But you hung it around your neck in the belief that it will

protect you or help you in some way, and that has made it something more special than when it was lying in the water. You invested it with a hidden force. You gave it power. It is now an amulet.'

My hand went to my throat. In the excitement of preparing for the journey, I had almost forgotten about my new amulet. But now that I had been reminded, I realised its power was humming inside me still. Not with the same force I had felt on the rock, but it was there all the same, ticking away like a dull toothache.

I wished I could talk to Carver about it, but something made me keep quiet.

'That pendant stinks,' said Crow. 'I don't know why you wear it, Wolf.'

Shadow seemed to agree with her because he growled at the dead crab and wouldn't sit on my lap.

I didn't dare open up to Crow about the amulet either, about the anger that was burning inside me like a fire. I knew she wouldn't understand.

Crow's problems were not solved with the help of the invisible world. She much preferred to use her spear and trusted arrows.

I smiled at Carver and said, 'I have seen simple pictures of beasts in a temple. Are they the work of people trying to connect with the hidden world too?'

'Oh yes,' replied Carver. 'In fact, my journey takes me to an underground cave full of the most wonderful images. Believe me, they take your breath away. They call it the Cave of the Dancing Animals. I am working on a standing stone circle close by. You can travel with me there if you want. I'd be happy to show you around the cave myself. It is vast. And then perhaps we can also find someone who can accompany you on the next leg of your journey, to the Island at the Centre of the World.'

'That would be great,' I said. 'If Crow agrees, I'd like to see this cave. Are the animals on the walls really dancing?'

'It will hold up the journey,' said Crow. 'But I have to admit, I'd like to see the cave too.'

We spent a night on the water, too exhausted to row any longer. Luckily, there was not even a breeze, allowing us to nap under our fur blankets without fear of the boat drifting too far off course.

At sunrise, we continued rowing and at last spied a coast that looked very much like the one we had left the day before. For a brief moment, my heart sank. Had we made a mistake and paddled in the wrong direction? But no, it was a different harbour that we docked at, with larger houses and pebbles on the beach instead of sand.

We said goodbye to the boatman and bartered some arrowheads for hot porridge and a place for the night. It was good to sleep on solid ground again. I woke up feeling refreshed and eager to continue our journey.

The next part of our travels took us through dark woods that gradually turned into flat land full of fragrant bushes and fast-flowing streams.

We went past villages built on the edges of lakes or sparkling rivers.

As we moved further south, the land became stonier, the soil lighter in colour. The people spoke a language different to my own and I could communicate only with signs. Carver, on the other hand, seemed to talk to everyone without a second thought. Everywhere we stopped, he was greeted as a friend.

I have no idea how long we trudged wearily, Shadow trotting happily ahead of us. But at last we came to a small village nestled at the foot of a dusty hill.

'This is where I'll be staying while I work on the new stone circle,' explained Carver. 'Tomorrow we'll visit the Cave of Dancing Animals.'

The next morning, we walked across wide, flower-strewn meadows and down into a valley.

'Look, there's the entrance to the cave,' said Carver, pointing to what looked like a wide crack in the rocks.

'Ha, is that it?' said Crow. 'If you hadn't pointed it out, I might have missed it completely.'

Carver smiled. 'I've heard tell that a long time ago, the entrance was kept a secret. Only a chosen few knew how to find it. That all changed when its power became known far and wide.'

Scooping up Shadow in my arms, I followed Carver through the crack in the rock. He'd brought three lamps with him, which we lit and held up.

I have no words to describe the beauty they illuminated. The cave was enormous, with walls disappearing into the distance. Every inch of rock was covered in drawings. Bulls and cows stared back at us with haunted eyes. Stags showed off gigantic antlers. Wild horses chased each other. There were geese and ducks and beasts I had no name for. Some of them did seem to be dancing.

'One of the horses has got long pointed horns,' I said to Carver. 'Are there really animals like that?'

'Perhaps that picture is meant to show us a spirit, or something from a dream that a shaman might have had. Most of these images are very old. Shamans say some are as old as time itself. Hold your lamp higher. Look, do you see? There are images even on the highest parts of the ceiling.'

'Yes,' I said. 'There are hunters painted up there, with bows and arrows. Look, some of them have managed to catch deer.'

'But who painted them?' asked Crow. 'And how did they get up there?'

'Hunters who wanted to make sure the spirits would grant them a good hunt,' replied Carver. 'Some also came to honour the spirits of the animals they had caught. They painted the pictures so that their spirits would still live on. That is why the pictures are dancing. Their spirits are free.'

We discovered a narrow tunnel flowing out of the main cave, its walls also covered in images. But these pictures were frightening. The animals were all bent out of shape. One showed a scowling shaman turning into a stag. His legs had already changed into hoofs but his hands were still human. The flickering light made his enormous dark eyes look real and alive, and angry. I felt the hairs rise on the back of my neck.

It suddenly dawned on me that I was trying to be a part of a very mysterious world, a world full of goodness but also dark secrets... and hidden danger.

And then I spotted something else that made my blood run cold.

It was a picture of a crab, like the one hanging at my neck. It too had an angry mouth full of ragged teeth.

And it was looking straight at me.

Chapter 7
A New Kind of Knife

I left the cave in a daze. The sight of the crab had shaken me. Why had someone painted it on the cave wall? Was it to thank the spirits for a generous catch? Or did it have a darker meaning? It had been painted in the scary tunnel after all. And the dead crab had appeared at my feet just after I had prayed to the sea-spirit in anger. I had assumed it was a gift. Could it also be a curse? Were the dark spirits expecting me to do something bad with it?

'Wolf, hurry up,' called Carver.

I turned to Shadow, pushing my thoughts of the crab to the back of my mind.

'Coming,' I said.

Back at the house where we'd spent the night, a crowd had gathered. It was mostly traders, stopping on their way to remote villages. Carver introduced Crow and I to a boy about our age. He was tall and thin but had powerful hands and very big feet.

'This is my friend, Ochre,' said Carver.

'I wasn't called Ochre at birth,' said the boy. 'My mother named me Owl on account that I was always staring. But now I trade in ochre, so that's what people call me.'

'Ochre is a bright colour that is used in paint,' explained Carver, as someone handed us a bowl of porridge. 'It's usually red but can also be yellow. The animals you saw in the cave were partly painted in ochre.'

'It's made from a special dust I dig up from the ground,' said Ochre, holding up his enormous hands. 'My land is famous for it. That is why I travel so far from home. People are willing to exchange rare goods for it.'

'Ochre's country is just across the sea from the Island at the Centre of the World,' explained Carver. 'It's called the Growling Island because there are mountains there that sometimes growl fiercely.'

'Do they really?' I asked.

'Don't be silly,' cut in Crow. 'Mountains don't growl. It's probably just a story people tell to frighten children.'

I shot Crow a dark look for scoffing but she ignored me.

'Perhaps, if Ochre is going back home, he could let you go with him. Then all you need do is find a boat that will take you to the Island at the Centre of the World.'

'I'd be glad of your

company,' said Ochre. 'My ancestors used to sell a lot of the red stuff, as I like to call it, to the people on the Island at the Centre of the World.'

'They say it's deserted,' added Carver.

'I heard only the spirits wander across the island now,' Ochre replied. 'Why you two want to go there is beyond me, but I've learnt not to ask strangers too many questions.'

'It's agreed then. We'd be delighted to go with you,' I said.

'And I can hunt along the way,' Crow offered. 'I promise your belly will always be full of stewed hare and deer meat.'

'I'm delighted to hear it,' laughed Ochre. 'I'm very good at finding seams of ochre but hunting is beyond me. I've never been able to catch as much as a mouse.'

That very same afternoon, we bid Carver goodbye and set off. Shadow leapt ahead of us, barking at every bird he saw in the bushes.

As we travelled south, I wondered what route

Rain had taken to the Island at the Centre of the World. Was he there already or was he, right now, treading the same rocky ground as me? Thinking of him, I clutched the stinking pendant at my throat.

My mind went back to the grimacing crab on the cave wall. I thought of its fierce eyes, looking directly at me and I shuddered. Then I remembered Rain ripping the bird-skull amulet from my neck. I heard him once again, lying about me, pretending to *be* me. The familiar anger rose in my throat. I knew I wouldn't rest until I had caught up with him.

Two moons grew full and waned. Crow hunted for us and always scouted villages to see if they were safe to spend the night. It was summer and I wore my furs only during the night. Despite the time of year, back on Great Island it would still be chilly. My mother would keep the fire going to heat the house. But here, the warmth was sticky and clung to your skin.

We came to a village where the people collected a sticky, yellow substance from the nests of buzzing insects. They called it honey. It was delicious in porridge and, Ochre told us, helped heal cuts and grazes.

Crow and I liked it so much we decided to take some with us on our journey.

'What will you barter me for it?' asked a woman who'd harvested a large batch that morning.

'A good flint knife,' said Crow. 'I am considered the best knife maker on my island. I assure you my knives never go blunt.'

'Ha,' replied the woman, slapping her thigh. 'What use have I for a stone knife?'

I looked at her wide-eyed. 'What do you mean?'

She drew a pointed knife from her basket. 'They still use flint knives where you come from? Look at this.'

She showed me her knife, whose blade gleamed a shiny salmon-colour in the sun. It had a very sharp edge that no amount of knapping could

get in flint. 'And it doesn't break as easily as the old knives either,' boasted the honey-dealer. 'It costs the earth, mind, but one of these can last you a lifetime.'

'May I...?' asked Crow, her voice a respectful whisper. I'd never seen her lost for words before. She took the knife and held it up to the sun so that its blade flashed like light on water. She passed her finger carefully along the edge of the blade, feeling its sharpness.

'What is it made of?' I asked.

'Bronze,' replied Ochre, who had come looking for us.

'Is that something dug out of the ground, like your precious dust?' I said.

'Sort of,' replied Ochre. 'Legend has it that two men placed rocks around their fire to hold a cooking pot. As the rocks grew hot from the flames, they released a strange liquid. From one rock came a red stream, and from another a shiny white one, like tears from the moon. The liquids ran together and, when they hardened, there was a new substance. It was a gift from the spirits of the earth. We call it bronze. Already it is used in many parts of the world to make tools, weapons and jewellery.'

I thought of my mother and father hacking at meat with a stone axe and making simple beads out of knucklebones. I'd always thought of Great Island as a modern place but, in reality, there was still much for my people to discover.

'I am sorry my flint knife is not good enough to barter,' said Crow, giving the woman her knife back.

'You can have some honey just the same,' laughed the woman. 'The spirits will look kindly on my kindness.'

'I shall not rest,' said Crow as we resumed our journey, 'until I have my own bronze knife.'

Chapter 8
Fire-Mountain

A few days later, we smelt the tang of salt in the air and soon after came to the coast. Here, too, there was a busy village full of boats.

Back on Great Island, people only got into a skiff if they absolutely had to. And very few people strayed far from the shore, for fear their skiffs might come apart in a storm. Here, it seemed people relished the idea of travelling across water, journeying from one land to another.

As we explored the waterfront, looking for the right boat, I could hear the jabber of different languages. It gave me a thrill listening to them and I wondered where all these people came from and what their lands looked like.

We found a boat that looked strong enough for our journey. Ochre haggled with the owner until the man nodded, smiled and shook his hands at the skies. This, Ochre explained, was a sign that the boat owner had asked the spirits to bless the deal.

After that we had a good look round the village, hoping to find out if Rain and Starlight had been there.

'Have you seen a boy my age, with thick hair tied behind the neck?' I asked a man bartering dried fish at the trading place. 'His hair is the same colour as mine. You might have noticed him if he came to trade supplies with you.'

The man looked at me blankly so Ochre translated.

'Tell him there would have been five older men with him,' added Crow. 'Their leader had his hair shaved back to the middle of his skull.'

'He says he did see a man like that a few days

ago,' said Ochre. 'He traded a goatskin for some fish.'

The man talked some more and Ochre translated, 'He says the man and his companions hired two boatmen to take them to my island. One of them was this man's son.'

The fish trader slapped the counter with a salted fish and spoke through gritted teeth.

'His son was promised a pot of salt for his work,' explained Ochre. 'He hopes the strangers will keep their bargain.'

Ochre and the fish trader kept talking but I wasn't listening. My heart was racing at the thought of catching up with Rain. I clutched my crab amulet. *He'll never escape me*, I promised myself. *I'll show him who's the most powerful between us.*

Ochre was eager to see his family so, once we'd checked our belongings were safely in our bundles and our water-skins were full, we set off.

'My island is the most beautiful place in the

world,' Ochre assured us as I coaxed a nervous Shadow onto the boat. 'Come on, Shadow. We'll be home before sundown and I'll get you a nice juicy bone straight out of Mother's cooking pot.'

'Poor Shadow nearly drowned once,' I explained. 'He still mistrusts the sea. I'll hold him in my lap.'

The sun was setting as we approached Ochre's island, turning the sea into liquid fire. A mountain loomed up ahead. It had a flat summit which seemed to be glowing from inside.

'One of your growling mountains?' I chuckled at Ochre.

'The loudest,' confirmed Ochre. 'That is Fire-Mountain,' he said.

'They say powerful spirits live inside it. Sometimes they fight and their fire-breath bursts out the summit and runs down the mountainside. My village lies right underneath.'

'In the path of the fire-breath?' I said.

'We have learnt to live with it,' laughed Ochre. 'Most of the time the glowing river stops before it reaches us.'

We docked just as it was getting dark and quickly made our way to Ochre's home. A woman rushed out to meet us. She was round and plump, with greying hair and dark, kind eyes.

'My mother,' said Ochre.

'Ochre,' cried the woman, drawing him into her arms. 'Ochre!'

I had no idea what she said next but I guessed it was a great welcome home.

'She says she missed me,' explained Ochre, disentangling himself from his mother. 'You'd think after all these years, she would have got used to me being away.'

His mother beamed and looked at me.

'This is my friend Wolf,' explained Ochre, nudging me forward. 'And this is Crow.'

Ochre's mother took our hands and led us indoors. Shadow followed, sniffing at the delicious smell in the air and wagging his tail furiously.

'Mother says she felt deep in her heart that I was coming,' said Ochre. 'She has prepared a feast.'

Ochre's father, who had also been a trader in his time, could speak a little of our language.

'Welcome to our home,' he said, inviting us to sit on pillows.

'They are on their way to the Island at the Centre of the World,' said Ochre.

'I too went there,' said Ochre's father. 'They say people from our land crossed to it a very long time ago and set up new homes. They built temples for the Goddess, grander than anywhere else in the world, and cleared the land for farming. They made precious salt and caught fish. My father and his father before him saw them many times, for they used to trade ochre with the people there. But now…'

'Now what, Father?' asked Ochre.

'The people disappeared,' replied the old man. He blew on his fingers. 'Like leaves on the wind. Some say they angered the Goddess and she turned them all into stones. Others say that a terrible disease killed them. Either way, no one lives there anymore. It is a place for restless spirits.'

Ochre's mother shivered and spoke to her son.

'She asks why you are going there,' said Ochre. 'It doesn't sound like a safe place for children.'

'Tell her we are following someone from my own village,' I said. 'He has something of mine that I must get back. I am not scared of the spirits. I am going to be a shaman when I grow up and, besides, I have an amulet to protect me.'

I showed her the crab pendant.

'It doesn't look very powerful to me,' said Ochre's father. 'But I do not know much about spirits and goddesses.'

'Well, he has me and Shadow to protect him,' offered Crow. 'I have my spear and my bow and arrow. I only wish I had a bronze dagger. We'd be much safer with it. The only problem is I don't have enough goods to barter for one.'

'That problem is easily solved,' said Ochre's father. 'I know the man who runs the ochre mine. Perhaps if you two offered to work digging up ochre, he would give you a bronze dagger in return.'

Chapter 9
Hard Work

I would have preferred to go after Rain right away but Crow had set her heart on that bronze dagger.

'It's not just for me,' she insisted. 'Imagine if we had bronze back home, on both our islands. Wouldn't it make life easier if we had weapons that did not break easily, if we had knives and axes that we did not have to replace all the time? If I could take a bronze dagger back to show my father, perhaps we can find out how it is actually made.'

'And Rain would not stand a chance against you with a weapon like that,' I said.

'Ha,' she said. 'Rain is no match for me even

if I was empty-handed.'

After our meal, Ochre's father took us to the mine where the ochre was found. It was a huge underground tunnel at the foot of the mountain. The man in charge took one look at Crow's strong arms and agreed to hire us right away.

'We ask only for a bronze dagger in return for our work,' said Crow.

Ochre's father spoke on her behalf. 'The man says you would need to work many moons for a new bronze dagger. But he has an old one you can have in return for a few days' work. It'll be the one dagger between you.'

'We accept,' said Crow, nodding and smiling at the man in charge.

He called out to a boy.

'This lad,' explained Ochre's father. 'His name means Eagle in your language. He is the son of the mine's owner and knows a little of your language. He will show you what to do.'

Crow and I followed Eagle down a rocky

corridor and round a bend, which blocked out the daylight. The only illumination now came from flaming torches stuck in the walls. Eagle handed us flint axes and showed us where to chip in the rocks for the precious ochre.

Crow and I soon got the hang of it and were digging away with the other children in the tunnel. It was hard work. By the time we stopped for a well-earned rest, I had painful blisters on my fingers. Dust got into my eyes and made them itch.

'Don't rub them,' warned Crow. 'You'll hurt your eyes.' She handed me a water jar. 'Poor Wolf. Don't worry. We only need work here for a few days. Then we'll get our bronze dagger and head on to the Island at the Centre of the Worl—'

Her words were interrupted by a distant rumble and a moment later, the ground started to shake.

CHAPTER 10
Buried Alive!

'The spirits are angry,' a girl nearby signed frantically with her hands. 'They are fighting.'

Her friends looked terrified and stepped away from the walls that were now releasing dust and gravel.

'Fire-Mountain is erupting,' signed Eagle. He shouted to the children, who quickly dropped their tools and gathered round him. I felt a warm hand in mine and looked down to see a little girl with wide, terrified eyes.

'Don't be scared,' I said with my hands. 'We'll soon be out of here.'

We were in a very deep part of the mine, in

a tunnel so low and narrow, only children could squeeze in. We crawled along it in a single line, like ants scurrying out of their anthill. At the end of the tunnel was a rope ladder that we had to climb one by one for fear of it snapping.

As I gripped it in my hands, I could smell an unpleasant scent in the air.

'It's Fire-Mountain's breath,' said Eagle. 'If it's penetrated this deep already, it means there are great cracks in the rocks above us. We need to hurry. The roof might cave in on us any moment.'

'You mean we'll be buried alive?' I said. My blood ran cold at the thought of a mountain collapsing onto me. I silently appealed to the spirits for help.

'Look,' said Crow, hauling me up through the hole. She indicated the ceiling where a thick, red-hot liquid was seeping through the cracks. 'Fire-blood.'

She turned to the children. 'Don't be scared,' she signed. 'The spirits will get us safely out of here. Isn't that right, Wolf?'

I nodded, hoping the children couldn't see the fear in my eyes. 'The spirits will never abandon good children like you.'

Eagle clapped to get everyone's attention. 'I know the way. Follow me and hold hands so no one gets lost. If you all do *exactly* as me, we'll all get out of here safely.'

We saw no adults as we meandered through a confusing maze of tunnels. I guessed they must have fled for their lives. The ground was littered with discarded tools and broken water jars.

The ground under our feet shook harder and harder until we felt a loud explosion that threw many of us to the ground. Eagle reeled backwards. There was a loud painful crack as his head hit against the rocky floor.

The children screamed.

Crow put her hand to Eagle's lips. 'He's still alive. I'll carry him.' Flexing her arms, she hauled the limp body to her shoulders.

'What do we do now?' I asked her.

'We go on,' said Crow firmly. 'Until we find a way out. Come on,' she signalled to the children with a nod of her head. 'Follow me.'

Faced with such determination, the children followed obediently. Before long, the mountain was shaking so hard we could hardly walk.

Then, without warning, the shaking stopped.

I held up my hands to ask for silence. 'The spirits have stopped fighting. Listen! Now's our chance to get out. Hurry up, everyone.'

We were all weak with thirst and hunger but there was an excited chatter among the children which spurred me on. If they weren't giving up hope, neither was I.

Crow, who was walking ahead of me, turned. 'There's been a rockfall. The tunnel's blocked. We'll have to go back.'

But the way back was blocked too, this time by a hissing river of fire-blood seeping out of the rock. Defeated, we all collapsed to the ground. I closed my eyes and appealed to the spirits. 'Please, please, save us.'

Even as I spoke, I had the feeling the spirits were not listening. They had well and truly abandoned me. My anger boiled out of me like the deadly fire-breath spewing out of Fire-Mountain. I threw my head back to scream and there, painted in a glowing white above me, I saw a familiar shape.

It was a giant crab like the one hanging around my neck and its eyes were mocking me. *You will die in here…*

'*I will not die!*' I screamed, picked up a rock and hurled it at it.

The rock didn't hit the wall. Instead it disappeared completely and I heard a hollow thud as it landed somewhere.

'Crow,' I called, scrambling to my feet. 'I think there's a hidden opening up here.'

'Where?' asked Crow.

I pointed to the yawning hole I could now make out in the crab shape. 'There! See it?'

'Yes,' said Crow, putting Eagle down. 'Someone must have painted that crab as a marker. Give me a hand up.'

She clambered onto my shoulder and hauled herself up. 'There's another tunnel here,' came back her muffled voice. 'I'll see if it leads anywhere.'

When she returned, there was a fierce glint of

triumph in her eyes. 'I actually felt clean air brush against my face. I think it might be a way out. Pass me the children one by one.'

I lifted each child into her outstretched arms.

'What are we going to do with Eagle?' I said. 'He's too heavy to lift.'

'Not for me, he's not,' replied Crow. She leapt down, heaved Eagle to her shoulders and clambered over me through the hole again.

I followed her, humbled by her show of strength and quick-thinking.

The tunnel turned and twisted like a giant snake until we could see a dull grey light ahead.

The children cheered and ran towards it.

We had found our way out of Fire-Mountain.

We were safe.

'Look,' said Crow, peering through a foggy daylight thick with ash. 'Isn't that Ochre's village down there?'

That night, after a good meal to celebrate our escape, I lay in Ochre's house and thanked the spirits for saving us.

Then I realised it wasn't the spirits that had come to our rescue. At least not the good spirits whose help I usually seek.

I thought of the crab with mocking eyes, and the stone that I hurled at it. It was the crab that had saved us. The crab and my anger. Not the good spirits of kindness and love.

Perhaps I needed to give in to anger more often. Perhaps it would help me triumph over Rain.

Chapter 11
Across the Sea

'Thank you for saving my son's life,' said Eagle's father. 'And the rest of the children. Usually the spirits send us warnings before they let Fire-Mountain breathe her deadly fire. The air smells strange for days. But yesterday, the mountain blew up without warning. We were lucky you were in the mine to lead the little ones to safety.'

He handed Crow a bronze dagger. Not the old weapon we'd been promised but a shiny new one, fit for a hero.

He turned to me. 'And this is some salt for you. It might not be as fancy as the bronze dagger but I can tell that you are not one for weapons.'

'Thank you,' I said, taking the pot. 'Salt is a precious thing. I shall use it wisely.'

One of the men whose children we had saved offered to take us to the Island at the Centre of the World. Early the next morning, we bid Ochre's family goodbye and left the village. It was a clear morning, the ash from Fire-Mountain having mostly cleared.

The sea was a vivid blue with patches of green here and there. It seemed to shine with a light of its own. Further away from the island, an enormous fish poked its head out of the water and seemed to laugh like a naughty child.

'That is a dolphin,' said the boat owner. 'The sea around here is full of them. Do you not have them in your land?'

'I have heard tell of them,' I replied. 'But I have never seen one before today.'

'They are friendly creatures,' continued the boat owner, whose name was Breeze. 'Some believe they are the messengers of the spirits. My children often manage to clamber onto their backs for a ride.'

I stared in wonder as the first dolphin was joined by others until there was a whole shoal of them leaping joyously around our boat.

It got hotter as the sun rose high in the sky. There was not a cloud to be seen. I took off my fur tunic.

'I wish we'd bartered these furs for lighter clothes,' grumbled Crow, doing the same.

Breeze shared out some food, then suggested Crow and I get some sleep. He handed us a large piece of cloth to use as a blanket. It would stop our skin from burning. My arms were already a bright red from the sun and I guessed my face was the same. As I stretched out under the cloth, looking up at the deep blue sky, my thoughts drifted back to Moon.

I hoped he was recovering from his illness. I wished he was here with me, to enjoy the marvels I was seeing, but mostly to give me advice. I had never needed someone to talk to as much as I did at that moment.

All my life, I had been aware that there were spirits guiding and influencing me. Wanting to be a shaman, I had always assumed that all spirits were good, that they only cursed and punished if you showed them a lack of respect. But now, having asked the help of an anger-spirit and got it, I was aware that there were two kinds of spirits. Bad ones and good ones. I had turned away from the good ones and sided with the bad ones. And the bad spirits had saved my life. Was I now in their debt forever? Had I become a bad person? Would anger rule the rest of my life?

I hoped not. I wanted to be good, to become the caring shaman I knew I could be. Perhaps, the good spirits would forgive my mistake and accept me once again.

With Crow snoring softly beside me, I removed the crab pendant from my neck and threw it into the sea. The moment I got rid of it,

I felt relief flood through me. Perhaps there was a glimmer of hope after all. Perhaps the good spirits would forgive me.

I dozed off with Shadow beside me, my dreams shifting from happy images of children on dolphins to frightening scenes of dark monsters reaching out from stormy waters.

'Wolf! Wolf! Wake up!'

I opened my eyes to see Crow glaring at me. 'You're awake already?' I said.

'I've been awake for ages, rowing for the both of us,' she huffed. 'Isn't that true, Breeze? Get up and help. My arms are getting sore.'

I sat up and reached for my oar.

'Oh look,' said Crow. She jabbed at the water with her oar and fished something out. 'Isn't this your disgusting, smelly amulet? You must have dropped it over the side of the boat.'

My heart sank when I saw the dead crab dangling from the oar.

'Throw it away,' I said. 'I don't want it anymore.'

Crow's eyes flashed as she unhooked the crab from the oar. It was a mean look I'd never seen before, and it made me shiver. Were the bad spirits working through her to get back to me? 'But you think the world of your little friend, the dead crab. You're always clutching it.' She looped the thong over my head. 'There. We can't have an apprentice shaman without an amulet now, can we?'

I wanted to rip the filthy thing from my neck but something told me it would not be the last I'd see of it. It seemed the bad spirits were not so easy to get rid of once you'd allowed them into your life.

Chapter 12
The Mysterious Island

The Island at the Centre of the World came into view shortly before sunset. It was just a strip of shimmering green land at first, but then it grew bigger and higher and I saw beautiful honey-coloured cliffs topped with lush trees. Its reflection wavered in the calm sea, making it look unreal, like something out of a dream.

As we got closer, the first stars came out even though it was not yet dark. It was eerily quiet as if the world were holding its breath, waiting for something to happen. There were signs that people had once lived and worked here. Wrecked boats lay on the shore. Derelict houses were clustered on top of the cliff. But there was no movement anywhere to suggest anyone still made it their home.

'No sign of Starlight and Rain,' said Crow. 'If they're already here, they're keeping well out of view.'

'Are you two going to be fine?' asked Breeze, as we rowed into a shallow sandy bay. 'I normally wait until the dawn to start on a return journey, but…'

'You need to get back home to your children,' said Crow tactfully. 'We will be fine, honestly.'

Breeze scowled up at the cliffs. 'This dead island is no place for children. Why don't you come back home with me?'

'Please, don't worry about us,' insisted Crow. 'Come back for us in seven days' time.'

Breeze fished in his bag and handed us the last of his food. 'Here, take this. It will keep you from going hungry until you catch something.'

'Thank you,' I said.

I stepped into the shallow water, holding Shadow in my arms. Crow followed. 'May the spirits watch over you, children!' Breeze touched his forehead with his finger as a way of saying goodbye.

We waved and watched him row away, whistling loudly to cheer himself up.

'It's warm,' said Crow. 'We should sleep on the beach tonight. Tomorrow, we'll start looking for Rain.'

'I'll make a fire,' I said. 'There's lots of driftwood scattered about, look.'

'No,' warned Crow. 'We can't risk Rain seeing the smoke if he is here. We'll eat the food Breeze gave us.'

After the meal, we found a sheltered spot under a strange tree with silvery leaves. I lay awake for a long time, listening to the sound of the waves nearby. Shadow slept soundly beside me.

When I did finally drift off to sleep, I had terrible nightmares. The beautiful sea turned a blood red and Rain emerged from it on the back of a giant crab. He had a bronze axe in his hands, which he threw skilfully at me, a grin slashed across his face.

Chapter 13
Abandoned Temples

I woke up to find Shadow licking my face. The sun was already shining. I had slept late. 'Shadow? Crow?'

'We're here, Wolf. Good morning,' said Crow. She was sitting at the water's edge, polishing the bronze dagger.

We had the last of Breeze's supplies for breakfast.

'I wonder if Rain is here already,' I said.

'We have to assume he is,' said Crow, 'which is why we have to be careful we're not spotted. There's at least seven of them, if Starlight's men all came here with him. There's only two of us. We'll only manage to capture Rain if we surprise them.'

'We haven't thought how we're going to get him away from the island without Starlight following us,' I said.

Crow shrugged. 'We'll have to make it up as we go along. Come on, let's start searching.'

Following a narrow path to the top of the cliff, we found the derelict village. Its empty houses were falling to bits, the roofs all caving in. Further inland, we came across open land that might have once been cultivated but was now overrun with weeds. Beyond it was a wood, thick with low-growing trees.

'There's a strange building in that clearing, look,' said Crow. We came out in a large circular space where the ground was covered with smooth, shiny stone. The building itself was built of a honey-coloured stone. It had a wide doorway in the middle, with large pottery urns on either side of it.

'This must be a temple,' I said. 'Let's go in.'

Coaxing Shadow to follow us, we found

ourselves in a warren of corridors that led from one circular room to another. In every room, silent figures carved from stone looked at us from the near-gloom.

'Are they spirits?' asked Crow.

'Perhaps,' I said. 'Or they might be images of people like you and me, or important people who must be remembered.'

In one of the larger rooms, we came across the figure of a very large woman. She had enormous legs that stuck out from under a dress with a frilled hem. Her chubby arms were folded against her chest. Her eyes were closed, giving her face a happy look.

'Is this She Who Sleeps?' asked Crow.

'Her eyes are closed,' I replied. 'But I don't believe she is asleep. I reckon she is just thinking.'

Looking at the stone figure gave me a strange feeling. I'd never seen anything like it. The pictures in Carver's cave were wild. They looked dangerous. This figure seemed to give out a sense

of peace. Looking at her, I could feel all the rage inside me starting to fade.

'Well, I don't think Rain has been here,' said Crow. 'There are no footprints in the dust. Come on, let's go and find a spring of fresh water. I'm thirsty.'

'You go,' I said. 'I'll catch up with you in a moment.'

Alone, I gazed at the figure again. Back home, even the hidden world was simple. You believed that everything around you had its own spirit. A faceless spirit! You treated everything with respect so that everything respected you back. Fear of angering the spirits kept you safe. But in the wider world, the hidden world seemed to have greater mysteries.

Without knowing why, I reached out and stroked the figure's face. 'Who are you?' I asked. 'Are you the image of someone important? Are you a spirit? Why do I feel at peace when I look at your face?'

'Wolf,' called Crow from outside. 'Are you coming?'

Reluctantly, I stepped away from the statue and went out into blinding sunshine. Shadow, who'd followed Crow, licked my knee and wagged his tail happily. He much preferred the sunny outdoors to the gloom of mysterious buildings.

Searching for water in the nearby woods, we soon found a stream. I was about to scoop some up, when I heard an angry buzzing in the trees.

'Did you hear that?' I asked Crow. 'There must be an awful lot of bees in the woods.'

'Strange,' she replied, peering around her. 'All the bees we've seen before were in open land.'

A moment later, there was a rush in the branches overhead. Someone dropped onto my back, wrapping their arms tightly around my neck. Swinging round, I could see that a second assailant was clinging to Crow. Shadow barked furiously but a third attacker, a girl, grabbed him and held his mouth shut.

Suddenly we were surrounded by children, swarming around us like bees round a honey jar. They buzzed angrily and jabbed at us with sharpened sticks, forcing us away from the stream and deeper into the wood. We reached a stone hut with an open door. The children shoved us in and we stumbled down a short flight of steps. They led us into a cave illuminated by a shaft of light coming through a hole in the roof.

A girl was sitting in the light, chewing on a fruit. She had a crown of leaves on her head.

'You are my prisoners,' she said. 'Get to your feet and bow.'

Chapter 14
The Bee Children

I stared at the girl wide-eyed. 'You speak my language.'

She nodded. 'My ancestors came to live here from the frozen north. We have passed our language down from father to son, from mother to daughter.' She indicated the children around her. 'Most of the others, they speak the language of their own ancestors: the people of the sunny lands. But they heard my language come from your tongue, which means you must have come from the north too. Who are you and what do you seek?'

'My friend and I are looking for someone from

my own land,' I said.

'You must want to find them very much if you've wandered so far from your home,' said the girl. 'Is it a lost relative?'

'No—' I began, but Crow cut in.

'Release us at once!'

The girl finished her fruit before speaking again. 'The men who came with you have opened the forbidden temple.'

'We came alone,' I said, 'just my friend, my dog and I. The men you mention did not come with us. They came before us.'

The girl looked from me to Crow. 'You did not arrive with the men who opened the temple?'

'No,' I insisted. 'We came looking for them. Their leader is a powerful shaman. A very dangerous man.'

'But the men had a boy with them. We saw him from the top of the cliff when they arrived. Are you not him?'

'I tell you I'm not,' I said. 'That boy is my

enemy. I came to capture him. He stole something from me which I want back.'

The girl leaned forward in the light so that shadows flickered across her face. 'What did he steal?'

'An amulet,' I said.

The girl looked from Crow to me. 'What do you know of the old prophecy?'

'We know nothing of prophecies,' snapped Crow. 'Let us go, and release our dog.'

The girl took no notice of Crow's demands. 'A long time ago, so the shamans of old taught us,' said the girl, 'this island was a happy place. They say that the Mother Goddess, the very spirit and guardian of the world, dreamt it up in her sleep.'

'What is a goddess?' I asked. 'Is it a spirit?'

'It is much more than that,' scoffed the girl. 'It is a truly powerful force. Only people in backward lands still believe in spirits. We who live in the warmth of the sun know the world and everything in it were made by gods and goddesses.

Our own island
rose from the sea to make the
Mother Goddess's dream came true.

'The Goddess had a sacred bird which used to sing in the morning to wake her up. She would let it fly high up in the sky. Its beautiful song carried on the wind and the people in other lands heard it in their dreams. They came in search of the song and discovered the island. They made it their home.

'The Mother Goddess adopted them as her children. She made the island rich and fertile for them. She put so many fish in the sea, they could catch them with their bare hands.

'Her work finished, the Mother Goddess lay down to sleep. The people built temples in her honour all over the island. They carved a statue of her sleeping and put it in the grandest temple of all. That way they would never forget her kindness.

'But as time went on, the people forgot how generous the Mother Goddess had been to them. They grew lazy and greedy. The farmers expected the crops to grow without working the land. The hunters killed animals just for the pleasure of it. Worst of all, the shamans wanted to become as powerful as the gods.

'They decided to wake up the Mother Goddess and demand she make them gods too. They made a spell to recite on the longest day of summer, when the magic of the world is at its most powerful.

'But when the shamans chanted the spell, something terrible happened. A bolt of lightning shattered the statue of the Sleeping Goddess. The shamans' vanity had angered the Mother Goddess.

'From that day on, the island was under a curse. The crops failed. The animals and the people grew sick. Traders stopped coming to the island, for fear of the curse.

'The people asked the Mother Goddess to forgive them. True, they had become lazy and greedy but it was only the shamans who had asked to become gods. Why should they suffer too?

'The Mother Goddess remained deaf to their prayers. The island continued to die. In despair, the people started to honour other gods in the hope that one of them might bless the island again. They abandoned the grand temple. The shamans were banished.

'Even then, the island never recovered. Most people left to start new lives in other lands. The few that remained behind, our grandparents, hid in the caves where the angry Mother Goddess would not see them. Even today, most of them only creep out under the cover of darkness. Only we children dare to leave the caves during the day. We call ourselves the Bee Children because we buzz as we move about, to fool the Mother Goddess into thinking we're bees in a hive.

'Slowly, the island is recovering from its curse. Our crops are starting to flourish again. Fish are returning to our waters. Perhaps the Mother Goddess has forgiven us at last. We hope that soon we will be able to live without the fear of disease and starvation again. But now there is a new danger.'

The girl paused and looked around her.

'What new danger?' I asked.

'Tell them, Sting,' said one of the children who had followed us into the underground room.

The girl, Sting, looked directly at me. 'There was one shaman who had not insulted the goddess. He was allowed to remain on the island. On his deathbed, he left us a warning. He said that when the Mother Goddess fell asleep, her singing bird flew away to the lands of the north. There it died and a shaman turned its skull into a powerful amulet. Its song had the power to wake up the Mother Goddess, who could not resist its beauty.

'The evil shamans did not believe they had made the Mother Goddess angry. The horrible things that happened on the island were not her punishments, just ordinary bad luck. One day, a young shaman, a boy with hair the colour of fired clay would bring the bird-skull amulet to the island and its birdcall would finally wake up the Sleeping Goddess. Then the shamans would ask once more to be made gods.

'It seems the prophecy is coming true,' said Sting. 'Shamans have arrived on the island. They have brought a boy with clay-coloured hair with them. The young shaman of the prophecy! They have already opened the forbidden temple. We cannot allow them to wake up the Goddess. It will just make her angry again and she will curse the island once more.' She looked at me. 'We thought you were the boy of the prophecy because you have an amulet hidden inside your tunic.'

'Do you mean this?' I said, pulling out the crab. 'I'm afraid this is only something I found in the sea.'

'Tell me the truth,' said Sting. 'What do you want with the boy the shamans brought with them?'

'He tried to kill me,' I confessed. 'I want to bring him to justice. And the girl who came with him. She's called Primrose, after the flower but— believe me—she helped him in his crime.'

'There was no girl with the shamans' party. Just five men and the boy.'

'I wonder what happened to her,' I said, turning to Crow who shrugged.

'So it's revenge you seek,' cried Sting.

'Yes, but there's more,' I said. 'The boy:

his name is Rain. I am Wolf and my friend here is Crow. Rain also stole the bird-skull amulet from me. It was gifted to me by a long-dead shaman. It allows me to have seeing-dreams. I am studying to be a shaman.'

The Bee Children all gasped as one. 'Then you are the true shaman of the prophecy,' said Sting.

'I swear to you I would never use the amulet to do anything bad,' I said. 'And I certainly wouldn't risk bringing a curse on innocent people. The power of the hidden world is not there to be abused. Rain, on the other hand, would stop at nothing to gain power.'

'Then we must help you get the bird-skull amulet back,' cried Sting, 'and you'll have to promise to take it away with you. You must get it back tonight. Tomorrow is the longest day of the summer, one of the most important days of the year. The shamans will try to wake up the Sleeping Goddess at dawn.'

Chapter 15
Rain

The birds had stopped twittering by the time we left for the forbidden temple. It was night but a full moon hung in the sky and there were more stars than I had ever seen. I don't think it really ever got dark on that island.

As we walked through thick undergrowth, more and more Bee Children joined us until we must have numbered at least a hundred. This time they buzzed softly, carrying their sharpened sticks.

'Will the grown-ups not join us?' I asked Sting.

She shook her head. 'You wouldn't get a grown-up near the forbidden temple if you promised them a lifetime's supply of food.'

'Do the shamans know this island is still populated?' asked Crow.

'We like to think that no one can spot a Bee Child unless she wants them to,' answered Sting. 'But I have to admit we are not as clever as we think. The shamans must be aware of us because they have men guarding the entrance of the forbidden temple.'

We came to the edge of the wood. Before us lay flat ground overrun with weeds. Beyond it stood a large building with a sloping entrance. I recognised it at once.

'It looks exactly like the temple in the land of

the Whispering Stones,' whispered Crow.

'You mean *that* temple is a copy of this one,' I said. 'The shamans who went to live in the north must have built a secret new temple to honour She Who Sleeps. Because it was hidden in the woods, they hung lamps in the trees to look like the bright stars on this island.'

Behind us, the Bee Children muttered amongst themselves. Sting quietened them down. 'I know many of you are a bit nervous being so close to the forbidden temple. Stay here. We'll call you if and when we need you. But make sure you're not seen.'

Leaving the Bee Children hiding in the wood, Sting, Crow and I crept through the weeds, Shadow following at my toes.

'We can't go in through the main entrance,' I said. 'Those guards would see us.'

'That is the back entrance,' replied Sting. 'The front entrance overlooks the sea on the other side. But we're using neither of the grand doorways. I've been inside the temple before. I couldn't roll away the massive stones at the grand entrances, so I found another way in.'

'How?' asked Crow.

'I went through the bleaching ground.'

I looked at her puzzled. 'The what?'

'An open space on the side of the temple. It's where they used to put the dead until the sun bleached their bones.'

I felt panic rise in my throat. 'Are there still bones there?'

Sting grinned. 'Yes. Why?'

'I think it's... disrespectful... to touch the

bones of the dead.'

'Ha,' said Sting. 'I'm sure the dead won't mind.'

'But…' I argued.

'Come on, Wolf,' sighed Crow. 'You'll have to make an exception this one time. So much depends on it.'

'So be it, then,' I snapped. 'Crow *always* knows best after all.'

Crow huffed through her nose, eyes flashing, but didn't say anything.

Silenced, I followed Sting through the weeds and round to the side of the temple. We clambered over a low wall and found ourselves in an enclosure littered with skulls and bones. I hesitated before taking another step forward. Shadow, sensing my fear, whimpered softly.

'These skulls,' I said. 'They should be facing the rising sun, not thrown around like this.'

'Wolf,' hissed Crow. 'Hurry up.'

I followed her and Sting along the temple wall until we came to a round stone leaning against it.

'This is the secret entrance,' said Sting. 'A tunnel. The shamans of old used to throw the bones through it.'

Crow helped her move the stone aside and she crawled in. I followed with Shadow.

The tunnel was lined with smooth polished stone and sloped downhill. I realised that what Sting had referred to as "throwing the bones" had probably been a much more dignified ritual. A skeleton, no doubt wrapped in cloth, would have been slid down to the tunnel to be received by shamans at the other end.

At the end of the tunnel was a round window that let in a glowing light. I squeezed up against Sting to see it properly.

Below us lay a circular room with slanting walls decorated with the same red spirals I had seen in Starlight's temple. Lamps hung from the ceiling. There was no one about. A large statue lay in the middle of the room. It showed a sleeping woman with enormous hips and tiny feet poking out of a frilled skirt.

'She Who Sleeps,' I whispered. 'Starlight's goddess.'

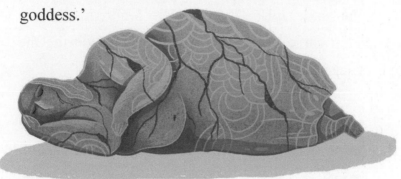

'And also the Mother Goddess,' said Crow, who had squeezed in beside me. 'Look, Starlight and his men must have put the statue back together again. You can still see the cracks.'

'What do we do now?' I whispered to Sting. 'Do we jump down and try and find Rain? The good spirits willing, he might still be asleep and I'll be able to get the amulet off him.'

'I think that's a good idea,' said Crow. 'Come on.'

But just then one of Starlight's men entered the room. We shrank back into the shadows, hoping he wouldn't look up and see us. The man, who was dressed in a flowing white robe, bowed to the statue and knelt on the floor before it. An eerie hum came from his lips. He was honouring the Sleeping Goddess.

The man was quickly joined by two more, preventing us from finding Rain. I hoped against hope they would stop their humming and go away. But it was not to be. The time dragged by and my legs went numb.

I was about to suggest a retreat back up the tunnel, when we heard the loud banging of a hand drum and Starlight swept into the room with the rest of his men, and Rain.

Dressed in a white robe covered in red spirals, his hair shaved back on his head like Starlight's, Rain looked very pleased with himself. My bird-skull amulet rested proudly on his chest. *He has what he has yearned for all his life*, I said to myself. *Everyone's attention.*

Seeing the amulet again made my blood boil.

I didn't care if it made me in debt to the bad spirits. This anger was too strong to suppress, and I knew it would be the only way to have the bird-skull amulet in my possession again. My hand clenched the crab around my neck. 'Let me get my bird-skull amulet back. Let me have my revenge.'

Only, it seemed the bad spirits had abandoned me just like the good ones. I was forced to watch, helpless, as Starlight's men danced around Rain and showered him with leaves from a basket. The drumming got louder and faster and, joining hands, the men formed a circle around the statue. A moment later, a shaft of dazzling sunlight reached through a hole in the wall and fell on the sleeping goddess.

'It is time,' cried Starlight. 'The first ray of sunlight is upon us. A brave new dawn for all.' He turned to Rain. 'Boy, hold up your amulet to the sunlight and recite the ancient spell I have taught you. Let the magic birdcall wake up the sleeping goddess. Quick, before the light of the new day passes from the room.'

Rain held the amulet up to the light. His voice echoed round the chamber as he recited the spell. The bird's eyes sparkled as if they were alive.

But that was it.

No magic birdcall came. No goddess appeared.

The light quickly faded as the sun rose higher. The men looked at one another in confusion.

'Boy,' growled Starlight. 'Tell me again how you got the amulet?'

Rain's face paled and he looked down at his big feet. I think up until now he hadn't even given the chance of failure a second thought. 'A-An ancient healer gave it to me.'

'An ancient healer?' said Starlight. 'Before, you said it was gifted to you by your father.' He turned to his men. 'The boy is clearly an impostor, not the child of the prophecy. That amulet is a fake, a useless skull. He has made fools of us all. Take him to the lower level. Tonight *he* shall be the sacrifice.'

Chapter 16
Wolfsong

As Starlight's men dragged Rain out of the room, I wish I could say I felt sorry for him but my heart was like a block of ice. It was numb. I could feel nothing for a bully that had made my life a misery.

Instead, I worried about the bird-skull amulet. I had to get it back. That was all that mattered.

'We must get out before we're discovered,' whispered Sting.

I shook my head. 'Not before I get my amulet back.'

'And we can't let Rain be sacrificed,' hissed Crow.

'Never mind Rain,' I snapped. 'I'm only

interested in the amulet.'

'He's from your village,' argued Crow. 'Your shaman's son. You cannot abandon him.'

'Crow is right,' said Sting. 'The boy might be a bully and a cheat but we can't leave him to his death.'

'He tried to kill me.'

'We need to find him to get your amulet anyway,' said Crow firmly. 'We'll rescue him in the process. He can face his punishment back home. Just as you always planned.'

I knew deep in my heart that Crow was right. My plan had been to take Rain back to Great Island with his father. There, I would get justice in front of the whole village. But that was the old Wolf's plan. The new Wolf wanted revenge. And I wanted my amulet back, which marked me out as someone special.

'Come on,' said Crow. 'We need to act before we're discovered.'

One by one, we dropped into the room and

Crow handed Shadow down to me. It was deathly  silent but we kept our eyes wide open for any sign of Starlight's men. We descended to a lower level; a warren of small rooms full of standing stones. Below it was yet another level with holes carved in the rocky walls. They were all full of skeletons, curled up like unborn babies still inside their mothers.

Crow suddenly put a hand on my arm. 'Do you hear that?'

I listened. Someone was crying softly nearby.

'Surely, it can't be… Rain?' I whispered. Shadow whimpered, disturbed by the sound of someone in pain.

We found a low doorway that led into complete darkness. The sobbing was louder here.

'Rain,' I called softly. 'Is that you?'

'Wolf?'

'I'll get a torch from one of the other chambers,' said Crow. She hurried back with the light and held it up. Rain was huddled in a corner of the room, his hands and feet tied securely.

Shadow whined again, trotted forward and gave Rain's face a comforting lick.

'Help me, Wolf, please,' Rain pleaded. 'They're going to kill me.'

I looked at his bruised face without pity. 'You deserve it,' I said. 'Didn't *you* try to kill *me?* Why should I feel sorry for you?'

I reached out to the bird-skull amulet and tore it from his neck.

However, the moment my hand closed around it, I felt it twitch. An image of Moon flashed before my eyes. His face was covered in ash, a sign of mourning, and in his ravaged eyes was the saddest look I had ever seen.

That sight of my mentor in such pain shattered the ice in my heart. In a moment, Rain was not the bully I had chased across so many lands and seas but my shaman's son. I saw him for what he truly was. A lost child from our village who needed help.

Moon's words of wisdom from back in Great Island echoed in my head: a shaman's duty is to help people, whether he liked them or not. Regardless of how they acted. He was not a judge, but a friendly guide.

'Crow,' I said. 'Lend me your dagger. I'll cut his ties.'

I cut Rain free and he struggled to his feet. Crow reached out to stop him from falling over.

'Hurry up,' whispered Sting. 'We need to get out of here.'

'Wait a moment,' I said. Hurriedly, I removed the shrivelled crab from my neck and replaced it with the bird-skull amulet. I would have nothing more to do with the dark spirits. I was on the side of the good again. I was home.

'Welcome back, Wolf,' said Crow. 'I've missed you—the *true* you.' She broke into a grin and I knew she was proud of me. 'Hurry up, apprentice shaman,' she said. 'We do need to get out of here before we're caught.'

We managed to reach the entrance to the tunnel before one of Starlight's men spotted us. The unexpected sight of four children and a dog made him jump. 'Master—' he began.

'Forget about the tunnel,' said Sting. She kicked the man's feet from under him and we rushed out of the room. By the time the entrance loomed up in front of us, the other men, including Starlight, were giving chase.

The moment we were outside, Sting gave out a piercing whistle. It was answered by a loud war-like buzzing and a swarm of Bee Children came pelting towards us. Starlight's men, who'd only just stumbled out into the sunshine, found themselves surrounded.

'Force them back into the temple!' called Sting. 'I'll meet you all in our meeting place tonight.'

'And where are *we* going?' asked Crow.

'To my parents' cave,' replied Sting. 'It's hidden away so no matter how hard the men from

the temple look, they will not find us. My mother will put ointment on your friend's bruises.

Sting's parents lived in a cave with spectacular views of the sea. They made us welcome with a meal and healing ointment for Rain.

Afterwards, he and I sat outside, watching the sunset.

'I want to say thank you,' said Rain. 'For saving my life. I… I am sorry for trying to kill you. I let jealousy blind me. Forgive me.'

I tried to detect a hint of insincerity in his voice but I could hear none. I was quiet for a moment, trying to sort out my own feelings. You would have thought an apology from your most bitter enemy would have filled you with satisfaction. But I only felt a shameful sadness.

'I am sorry too,' I said. 'I let my pride and anger blind *me*.'

'I need to make amends with my father,' said

Rain. 'I will willingly come home with you to face judgement by the elders. Let us be friends.'

We stood up and clasped hands, like chiefs sealing the peace between two warring tribes.

'I think I shall sleep soundly for the first time in moons,' said Rain, in a softer voice than I'd ever heard him use. 'How long do we have to wait for the boatman to fetch us? I can't wait to be away from this island.'

'A few days,' I replied.

'That's not long,' he said. 'Though I feel safe in this hidden place, my heart is ready to go home. Thank you again, Wolf. Goodnight.'

He went back inside the cave, leaving me alone with Shadow. It was not yet dark but enormous stars already glittered in the sky. The air was heavy with the scent of shrubs and flowers.

'I think this is the most beautiful place the Mother Goddess ever made,' I whispered to Shadow.

He licked my hand to show he agreed and rested his head on my lap. I scratched between his ears. For the first time in a long while, my heart was full of peace. I had made the right choice. Forgiveness over revenge. Good over bad.

There was only one thing in this whole saga that still puzzled me: was the prophecy true? Was a boy with a bird-skull amulet meant to wake up the Sleeping Goddess? And, most curiously, was the boy with the bird-skull amulet... *me?*

The spirits had led me on this journey. Had they led me here for a reason other than capturing Rain? If so, the spirits really did move in mysterious ways.

With Shadow snuggled on my lap, I started singing my Wolfsong. I sang to the good spirits, to the goddess and asked them to show me what to do next.

And that's when the bird-skull amulet twitched against my chest.

Wolf's journey will continue in

The WOLF'S SONG

AUTHOR'S NOTE

Like all the other books in the *Wolfsong* series, *The Mysterious Island* is a work of fiction. Wolf, Crow, Rain, Sting and all the other characters are the product of my imagination. Many of the places, however, are real.

The Cave of the Dancing Animals is inspired by the caves at Lascaux in southwest France. Over six hundred paintings cover its walls and ceilings, some of them over nineteen thousand years old. Lost to the world for thousands of years, the cave was rediscovered in 1940. An eighteen year old mechanic called Marcel Ravidat was walking in the vicinity when his dog, Robot, fell down a hole. Trying to rescue him, Marcel and his friends stumbled across the entrance to the hidden caves.

After experts had studied the paintings to discover their age and meaning, the caves were opened to the public in 1948. Over the years, the pictures started to deteriorate, so the complex was closed up and the paintings restored. Today you can visit a nearby exhibition that shows you copies of some of the breathtaking artworks.

Fire-Mountain is based on Mount Etna on the island of Sicily. Volcanic activity in the area is believed to have started some 500,000 years ago. The result is the second highest mountain in Italy and one of the most active volcanoes in the world. The volcanic ash spewed from Mount Etna makes the soil in the surrounding area very fertile. There are farms and vineyards all around its lower slopes.

The Mysterious Island is Malta. One of the smallest places in the world, it also has one of the oldest cultures. Sitting in the Mediterranean sea between Europe and Africa, Malta has been a link between the two continents. Different peoples set up homes there, building some of the most jaw-dropping temples in the world.

The first one that Crow and Wolf find is today known as Tarxien Temples. It is actually a complex with three main buildings. The first was constructed around 3000BC. Large stone rollers left on site show how the builders moved the massive boulders for the walls. For unknown reasons, the temple was abandoned at the end of the Stone Age but used as a crematorium during the Bronze Age.

The temple where Rain is imprisoned is called the Hypogeum. That means 'underground' in Greek because most of the temple is below ground. It was used by the early inhabitants of Malta between 3500BC and 3000BC when the nearby Tarxien Temples were built. It is famous for its oracle room where a person's voice was amplified and echoed around the entire temple. Many funerary objects were found in the Hypogeum, including statues of She Who Sleeps, today called the Sleeping Lady. It is one of the most famous prehistoric artefacts in the world.

DISCUSSION POINTS

Wolf and many of the other characters face **conflict** time and time again in *The Mysterious Island*.

- What kind of conflicts do we see? Are they always between the "good" and "bad" characters?
- How do the characters deal with these conflicts?
- Are there any conflicts that could have been avoided? If so, how? Likewise, was it important that the characters experienced them regardless?

Wolf and Crow encounter **bronze** for the very first time in the story.

- How do you think people's lives changed by using bronze instead of stone?
- Bronze is made from combining copper and tin, but how do you think people in the Neolithic era imagined bronze was created?

- What other inventions in the Bronze Age do we still use today?

Wolf struggles with **anger** in *The Mysterious Island*.
- How does he overcome this?
- What does Wolf's experience with anger teach us about its consequences? What happens when he gives in to his anger too much?
- Who else experiences anger in the book? Why do they feel angry?

Forgiveness is something Wolf also learns and experiences during his journey.
- Who does Wolf forgive in this story, and why?
- Is forgiveness an easy thing to do? Why or why not?
- Why do you think forgiveness is important in the story?